TREATED

AS A
JEW

BURT JAGOLINZER

Visit our website at www.StillwaterPress.com for more information.

First Stillwater River Publications Edition

ISBN-10: 1-950-33900-9
ISBN-13: 978-1-950-33900-6

1 2 3 4 5 6 7 8 9 10

Written by Burt Jagolinzer
Cover Design by Kody Lavature
Published by Stillwater River Publications, Pawtucket, RI, USA.

FOREWORD

Burt Jagolinzer lived through a portion of World War II, while growing up in Providence, Rhode Island.

He was one of three boys in his family. His father served as a government air-raid warden during most of the conflict.

Stories about the military campaigns and individual war-time experiences surfaced regularly during and after the end of the war.

Burt and his family realized, like many Americans, how lucky they were to have come through this horrible era safely. Mr. Jagolinzer decided to pen a story that could have happened during this terrible conflict.

MEMORIALIZED

The author has chosen to memorialize his lost families in Europe, eliminated during the Second World War by Nazi Germany.

He and his American relatives had uncles, aunts, cousins, and more captured, tortured, and killed during that ungodly period.

Our world will never forget the multi-millions whose lives were brutally taken during that terrible conflict.

MAY THERE NEVER AGAIN BE SUCH A WAR, UPON OUR EARTH

CHAPTER ONE

Ivan Kranofsky was born in Bruzgi, Poland in December of 1928. His father Luz worked for the Polish National Railway (PNR) in nearby Belarus as manager of incoming coal, which during the 1930s, was considered to be excellent, safe employment.

Luz would purchase enough coal from local sources and make sure that deliveries took place at the needed rail locations, and he ensured the deliveries were on time.

Young Ivan grew up practicing the Catholic Church values of the day. He attended church services regularly with his mother and younger sister Anna.

Ivan's closest friend was Hyman Goldenstein, who lived two doors down the street.

Hyman and Ivan were the same age and they schooled together at the local public building that also included the fire and police stations.

Both boys had eyes on Brenda Cropsky, an adorable classmate who lived on the other side of town.

Brenda's young smiling face complimented her large brown eyes. Her freshly-coiffed dirty-blonde hair accentuated her youthful teen figure. She would speak near-perfect Polish language regularly to the boys.

It was now January 1939 and Hitler's German aggression began to sweep through portions of Europe.

Poland began preparing for a possible war against the Germans.

The Polish military was quite outdated and relied upon equipment and knowledge from the First World War, which ended in 1918.

Yet, many felt that they still had enough strength to stop the Germans if they chose to attack. And

negotiations with Germany showed initial promise to the Poles.

They were hopeful that war could be avoided.

But on August 23, 1939, Hitler secretly forged a
pack with Russia's Stalin to conquer and divide
Poland.

Hitler authorized the invasion of Poland ten days
later on September 1st, 1939.

His excuse to the world for the invasion was, "To
defend Germany".

As a result, Britain and France immediately de-
clared war on Germany.

Tanks and heavy superior equipment raced into
the heart of Poland. The German air force bombed
the cities and air strips quickly destroying the
Polish response.

The Poles met the German tanks with an outdated horse-driven infantry and were quickly beaten in a massacre.

The Nazis were told to eliminate anyone who defended or resisted the invasion movement.

They worked their way into the heart of the country rounding up Jews and others who they suspected wouldn't welcome them.

Many were shot on the spot. Others were taken away and eliminated later.

Forces were about to approach Bruzgi where Ivan and his family resided.

The Kranofsky family didn't know what to do. They were horrified.

CHAPTER TWO

The Gestapo-trained units systematically approached each village and removed the habitants while also destroying their homes and facilities.

Their ultimate goal was to select useful slave labor and then level the country. The rest of the people were to be eliminated or sent to concentration camps that had been quickly set-up in occupied Poland and elsewhere.

On the third day of the invasion, Ivan and his family were visited by a Gestapo group that broke down their front door. They grabbed Ivan's father Luz and brought him outside and shot him in the head.

His mother and sister Anna screamed violently as they were taken away.

Ivan was beaten and pushed into an armored vehicle.

He looked back as they set his house on fire with gasoline.

The Gestapo group continued down the village street.

Nazi-Wehrmacht soldiers were everywhere. Ivan could see that Bruzgi had been totally conquered.

He was alive but had a broken nose and head wounds. Blood was running down his shirt and trousers.

Ivan was shaken to the core having lost his father and possibly his mother and sister. He had no idea where he was headed or whether he would survive.

The armored vehicle moved quickly through the ruined village and countryside.

CHAPTER THREE

The armored vehicle came to a bumpy stop. Two soldiers came to the back of the vehicle and released the locked gate.

Speaking Polish, one of them commanded Ivan to come forward.

Ivan moved slowly forward, to the edge of the truck bed.

"You are to be processed," he yelled.

The two soldiers quickly grabbed Ivan by the arms and lifted him to the pavement.

"Why am I being processed? And what about my mother and sister?" Ivan asked.

"They will answer your questions inside this building," the soldier replied.

The two soldiers escorted him to the front of the building.

This building had once been a Catholic Church and it had been heavily bombed by the invasion force. A portion remained intact, and they had already put a swastika on the entrance that had survived the bombing

A guard stood by the doorway with a combat rifle by his side.

The two soldiers spoke in German and gained entrance to the structure.

Inside the church, three broken pews were being used for individuals waiting to be processed.

The two soldiers pushed Ivan into a pew that was already full of many depressed and unhappy individuals.

It was apparent that he was to wait there until he was called into the priest's office which appeared to have been undamaged during the air strike.

About twenty people were seated in the pews.

Ivan thought that this would give him time to relax, observe, and consider any calculated move that he might undertake.

He sat there, a bit relieved for a while, but became increasingly concerned about his future and survival.

The woman next to him had obviously been mishandled and beaten, and her lip was bleeding. Her clothes were ripped, her hair was disheveled, and her right arm was wrapped in cloth. She sat looking down in horror.

"Do you speak Polish?" Ivan asked.

"Yar, but I have been warned not to speak to anyone. They have my children and will destroy them if I don't follow their instructions," she replied.

"Then just nod your head or move it to answer yes or no," he requested.

"Yar," she returned.

"Good. Where are you from? Is it Belarus?" he began. She nodded.

"Did they destroy all of your city?"

"Yar," she responded without nodding.

"Do you know of any way to escape either now or in the future?"

She moved her head from right to left.

There came a violent scream. It had apparently come from inside the office.

The door opened, and two well-dressed special agents dragged the body of an elderly woman out of the church.

In fluent Polish one of them spoke, "Mrs. Corrine Zuppowitz is next."

The woman next to Ivan rose from her seat and moved slowly toward the open office entrance.

CHAPTER FOUR

One by one the captives in the church pews were called into the closed office. Several screams were heard and two were apparently shot during the interrogation process.

Most came out of the office under guard. There were soldiers waiting just outside to take each of them somewhere, taking their instructions in German.

Four new individuals had arrived during Ivan's wait.

One woman had a shaved head and wore a prison-type dress. She wore glasses with smashed lenses and was crying.

Ivan now knew, for sure, that his integration was about to be difficult. Finally, after the office door opened and the captive was removed in handcuffs, there came a shout.

"Ivan Kanopsky," called the soldier.

Ivan rose from the pew and slowly moved toward the office entrance where the soldier was standing, with his papers in hand.

The priest's office was just the way he had remembered it.

There was an ornate desk, hand-carved by a veteran craftsman, with the same high-back chair that the priest would sit in placed behind the beautiful desk.

Pictures of Jesus and the local bishop were still on the walls. The nearby file cabinets were smashed, and paper and files were scattered on the floor in several directions.

He was told to sit in a broken chair poised in front of the desk.

There were three well-dressed men in the room leaning against the far walls.

The interrogator wore a ranking Wehrmacht uniform that appeared to be highly decorated. He was a young man, probably about thirty years old, with deep brown eyes and a wide authoritative look. Speaking in broken Polish, he began.

"You are a Jew."

"No, I am Catholic, and this was my church," Ivan responded.

"No, you are a Jew. We know this from your friend Hyman Goldenstein who we processed yesterday," he continued.

"No, it is a lie. I am Catholic and not a Jew," Ivan countered.

"Because of your friendship with Hyman, and his words, we will process you as a Jew. How old are you?" he asked.

I will be twelve in October," Ivan returned.

"Because of your young physical body, we will put you to work. You will be well cared for," he exclaimed.

"What about my mother and sister?" Ivan asked.

"They have been processed. Your mother might not live, but your sister will probably be saved for our officers if she is pretty."

"Take him away," were his final words.

Two of the well-dressed men grabbed Ivan by the arms and escorted him outside where guards forced him into a squad vehicle.

He heard them receive their orders in German.

The driver saluted and jumped into the vehicle.

The back doors were locked.

Ivan began to cry for his mother and sister.

He also feared for his own life, not knowing where he was being sent or what his future was to be.

CHAPTER
FIVE

The vehicle came to a stop in front of the Belarus Railroad Station. Ivan's father Luz had worked there for some thirty years. He had become an executive, attaining the title of procurement officer.

Ivan had visited his father many times at his office just above the ticket window area.

As a youngster he had climbed the steps from the wooden floor below directly into his father's busy office.

Today he didn't know what to expect at the station.

The station was now occupied by the Nazis and soldiers were placed all around the building.

An identifying Swastika was very visible above each entranceway.

Smoke from trains seemed to be all around. The noise of their engines filled the air. Activity appeared to be very brisk at this station.

Ivan was taken abruptly from the vehicle by two new guards. The sedan was closed, and it quickly left the station area.

The guards were aggressive and showed it in their faces that they were not very happy to be doing what they were obviously ordered to do.

Ivan was pushed through the entrance door into the passenger arrival area.

He was given a cup of water by a woman in a dirty black dress who approached him as he was forced to sit in a passenger-rung aisle nearest the outer door that led to the railroad tracks outside.

The two soldiers left him and returned outside.

There were possibly one hundred people in the building. Most of them appeared to have been beaten or violently processed.

Among the group were women, children, and elderly couples.

To Ivan's amazement, he spotted Hyman Goldenstein in the very next aisle.

There were women soldiers scattered around the room leaning against the walls. They were well-dressed in black German uniforms and they carried pistols on their belts.

It was obvious that they were to keep these people under control.

Ivan was anxious to reach Hyman to find out how he had arrived here, and what he might know about where they would be going.

He asked the man next to him if he would exchange places with him.

The man, who was disheveled and without shoes, had a large dirty- white bandage across the left side of his head. He agreed to move for him.

The switch brought him closer to Hyman.

An elderly woman was next in the way toward his goal.

She could not speak. Her mouth had been beaten and her voice had been damaged and it limited her ability to converse.

Her coat was in rags and was ripped at the collar.

She had overheard Ivan's request from the last individual and nodded her head to Ivan, indicating
that she would help him, too.

The lady stood up and made the change happen.

Ivan was now within talking range of connecting
with Hyman.

"Hyman, it is me Ivan. Are you okay?" he asked

Hyman turned toward him and spoke softly. "My
parents were shot in the street before me. They
grabbed all the family treasure and food. Then
they slapped me with a whip until my left eye
was destroyed. I cannot see out of my left eye.
Perhaps the marks on my head might go away
some day if I'm lucky," he responded.

Hyman was visually a mess and was in a deeply
depressed state.

"My father was killed and my mother and sister
were taken away. I don't know whether they will
survive. Where are we going? Do you have any

idea? And, by the way, they said they will treat me as a Jew," Ivan explained.

"I overheard one of the soldiers say we were headed for a concentration camp somewhere in rural Poland. They spoke in German which I was able to understand because my mother spoke German during family conversations in our house over the years. If this is so, maybe we will be alright after all. And you are not a Jew. Don't they know that," Hyman answered.

"The processor told me that because of my friendship with you, I will be treated as a Jew. I don't think he did me any favors," Ivan continued.

"At least we may be placed together in the future. I think that might be important for both of us," Hyman returned.

A Nazi Officer entered the building and blew a whistle.

He demanded all to stand.

"You will all be transported by the railroad NOW!" he shouted.

CHAPTER SIX

All one hundred prisoners who were in the passenger waiting area were quickly pushed through the outer door leading to the tracks.

Waiting for them outside was a train with some twenty box cars filled with screaming captured men, women, and children. They had obviously been taken from other parts of Poland but were now headed for the same destination. They had been squeezed into each box which was locked from the outside.

One box car was opened loudly, and a whistle began the quick movement of the waiting captives into the open box.

Ivan and Hyman were able to stick together during the boarding.

Hyman found a small crack in the wall of the box, just to the left of the entrance area. Ivan pushed his way over to stand next to Hyman.

The box car continued to fill up.

It became apparent that all one hundred or so would be forced into this basic box whether they wanted to or not.

Somehow all the captives were squeezed inside, and the heavy rolling door was closed and locked.

Many screams began to arise from within the group.

They now knew that survival could become very difficult.

The stuffed car had limited oxygen and it appeared that not all were going to make it to wherever the train was destined to take them.

Fortunately, Hyman and Ivan had valued being near that crack in the wall of the box car.

They realized that the air and or oxygen from that crack might be a life saver. Most of the others didn't know that the crack even existed.

The train began moving. It picked up speed and the box cars swayed with the quick turns and abrupt movements from the fast-directed Nazi commander at the controls.

Individuals in the box started climbing upon each other to produce room to get basic movement.

There was no food, no water, and no facilities. Several people pushed away from a corner, and it became the only place for urine and other releases during the trip.

The smell and embarrassment that came from that area was beyond anything these people had ever endured.

They had no choice but to make the best of the terrible conditions and prayed to God that they could somehow survive this unforgiveable situation.

Several people prayed loudly for God to take them quickly to their destination. Many began to doubt they would survive at all.

The train rambled on for over twenty hours without stopping and with no food for anyone

Finally, the train began to slow and then stop. It became apparent that they had reached their destination.

CHAPTER
SEVEN

There was silence. Then loud German commands were shouted followed by the noise of the opening of some of the box car doors.

One by one the cars were unloaded, starting at the end of the train.

They could hear the commands, people screaming, and the occasional firing of a shot or two.

Some twenty minutes later, the guards arrived at Ivan and Hyman's box car.

Finally their door was rolled opened.

Six Nazi troopers appeared shouting out instructions.

Those who could walk came out in poor condition. They were barely alive.

Ivan and Hyman were in a reasonable shape, yet weak from thirst and lack of food like the others.

Only about half of the passengers in the crowded box were able to come out on their own. Two Nazi troopers climbed in to get the rest.

They quickly returned, helping four or five to the box's edge who were quickly brought to the pavement by other troopers.

The two troopers returned to the interior of the car. There were five shots heard. The troopers then left the box car immediately.

It became apparent that several individuals within their car had perished during the trip and that they decided to eliminate the others who could not help themselves.

Another whistle blew and three slave-like looking men arrived, heads shaven, dressed in striped, worn, and dirty clothes. They were immediately ordered to climb into the car, remove the bodies, and clean the box.

Standing on the side of the tracks were over a thousand individuals – men, women, and children – beginning to go through an interrogation process.

One man began to run away in the opposite direction. A Nazi guard opened fire and killed him instantly.

Ivan and Hyman got the message.

They waited in line another fifteen minutes until it was their turn to be evaluated.

Hyman stepped forward first.

A young Nazi was asking questions in broken Polish. "What is your age?" he demanded to know.

"I am twelve, please," he responded.

Another ranking officer shouted, "You are to go to the left side!"

Hyman was pushed to the left.

Ivan moved forward, "I am twelve also, but I am not a Jew."

The ranking officer shouted, "You are to go to the left side."

The young Nazi smashed Ivan's face with the back of his hand. "You will die as a Jew, you swine. Now move on."

Ivan and Hyman stayed together.

A cup of soup awaited them when they reached the inner fences that encircled a make-shift village ahead of them.

The potato soup was terrible, but when in hunger, most anything becomes a blessing to one's body.

They were to follow the line that stretched out before them. The line brought them to a shed with an open window.

A clean pair of work clothes were thrown at each of them.

The clothes were not new. They had been worn by previous captives who had been eliminated, the clothes reprocessed, and once again distributed. No special sizes were even considered.

They were assigned a building and were told to remove their personal clothes but were not allowed to put on the work clothes.

Inside the wooden building, bed bunks scattered in all directions.

They were told to select one, undress, and wait.

Ivan and Hyman chose bunks next to each other at the far right of the entrance.

They were ordered to stand there, in the nude, and await further instructions.

CHAPTER EIGHT

A young officer came through the entrance and demanded that they all march behind him. They were led to an outdoor shower where cold running water was running continuously.

One by one they entered the cold shower and then were told to return to their inside bunks.

There, they were directed to wipe dry with a small clean towel that had been distributed to each bed while they had been gone. Their personal clothes had been taken away.

After being allowed to dress into the prisoner's clothes, they were marched to an open spot where trained inmates were ordered to shave everyone's hair. (The hair was being transported to other areas for use in making pillows and other items.)

Ivan and Hyman were now shaven and dressed in their prison attire.

A man three bunks away from them refused to get into his prison clothes. He was taken out in the nude and tied to a post. He was found dead the next morning.

A young German soldier was assigned to their building. His name was Heinrich, but the inmates began calling him Heiny.

Heiny seemed to be a nice guy, but he made it clear that he must follow directions from above. He spoke broken Polish.

One hour later they were filed out of the building and ushered into columns in front of the entrance.

Heiny was told to pick ten individuals for immediate duty. He quickly pointed to the first ten men standing in front of him. They stepped forward.

They marched off with a group of other appointees.

The ten from their building never returned.

Two days later, ten new prisoners arrived to take their beds.

During the first morning, Heiny pointed at Ivan, Hyman, and one other boy to follow him.

They were brought into a building where shoes were being stacked almost to the ceiling on both sides of the room.

A prisoner had been put in charge. He spoke in fluent Polish, "We are to clean and take the laces out of each shoe, then put the shoes into the carts that were outside the closed door. The laces are to go into this large box. Please take your time, as this will continue to be our duty. My name is Boris. I have been here for nearly two years."

It appeared that Ivan and Hyman had found a good place to work, just by luck.
The third man from their barracks was named Felix.

Felix had been in Belarus when he was seized. He claimed he had been a fireman-in-training.

During the third day at work, Felix began taking some of the laces and putting them in his inside pocket.

Hyman caught him doing it and asked him why he was taking them. His quiet remark was encouraging.

"They may be useful in the future if a chance to escape should come our way."

Their typical work day started around dawn and lasted until dark.

Most of their dinners consisted of a boiled potato, one slice of dark bread, and a cup of water.

Since there were no lights of any kind, most prisoners went to sleep right after dark.

They would chance talking to each other once in bed, but only at a low breath. Most of the talk was complaints.

One individual spoke of God's chosen power and how he must have selected them all for a good reason. He reminded them all to, "never give up."

Never give up became a motto for Ivan and Hyman. They realized that no matter what was to come before them, they must keep a positive attitude somehow–and not give up.

It wasn't long before several individuals in their building were showing signs of depression. Their future was not good.

The Nazi's were instructed to pick out those individuals and work them to their deaths.

The atrocities around the camp were increasing.

A small group had tried to escape and were caught. They were hanged before the entire camp first thing the next morning.

Heiny began telling his inmates that the war had been going quite well and that Germany will rule the world shortly.

No other information from the outside came to them at that time.

All the prisoners began to lose weight and energy, struggling to complete the labor that was required of them each day.

Many who faltered were shot on the spot, others were taken away and eliminated.

The numbers in their building kept getting smaller and replacements came to fill the beds.

Heiny kept praising the three that worked in the shoe room. "You probably have the best job," he explained.

"But you, too, will have to face punishment soon. I will not be able to protect you forever, but I will try my best," he added.

Sure enough, after nearly three months in the shoe room, things began to change.

Heiny had kept his word. He was told that more laborers were needed at another location and that transportation would become available soon.

He volunteered the three young boys for the duty.

Without further delay they were accepted, and Heiny was told to prepare them for movement the next day.

Heiny told the boys, "this camp is to be removed very soon. Most of the prisoners here are to be killed. I have arranged for you to go to another location. There is no promise for your safety there, but it is a chance you must take, without choice. I wish you luck."

The next morning, they were loaded onto a train heading north.

CHAPTER NINE

This train had space for the boys to sit down inside a passenger car loaded with German soldiers and other individuals in prison uniforms and shaved heads.

The soldiers were watching them, and they had been assigned to various groups.

The boys struck up a conversation with two other young individuals seated across from them.

"Do you know where we are going?" Ivan asked.

"No. I am here because I am being punished for not eating their terrible soup yesterday," the first boy responded.

"And I peed on the floor of our bunk house," added the other.

Ivan continued, "The three of us were working in a shed sorting-out shoes and laces. But our guard sent us here because the whole camp was to be destroyed. He said that where we are going will give us a better chance to survive. That's all we know."

"My name is Ivan, and their names are Hyman and Felix. What are yours?"

"I am Shloma and this is Smell. We are from outside of Krakow in a suburb called Pietry. We think that maybe we are lucky as the big city people are to be totally eliminated, according to a Nazi guard we talked to just yesterday."

Hyman responded, "I think the five of us should try to stay together and see what we can do to help each other survive."

"Yes, we have nothing to lose. Often, more than one head can offer important choices that could be overlooked," said Shloma.

The five smiled at each other. Smiling had been very difficult during these terrible days.

After nearly six hours of travel, the train began to slow down. The engine stopped, and they heard whistles and noise coming from outside.

The soldiers began leaving the passenger car and the prisoners were told to follow.

When they departed the train, several Nazi officers were waiting, sending the prisoners in several different directions.

About a dozen, including the five boys, were herded to the right side of the train platform.

Near them stood two imposing young Nazi soldiers who immediately led them to a waiting large truck. They were told, in broken Polish, to get into the back of the vehicle.

The chain and door were locked. The vehicle began to move.

After twenty minutes of traveling, the loaded truck stopped. It appeared they had reached their destination.

They were told to disembark from the vehicle.

To their surprise, it was quiet. There was no noise, no whistling, and no sounds of war.

They wondered. Where were they? And why were they here?

CHAPTER TEN

Three prisoners, each with shaved heads and dressed in prison uniforms, helped them down from the vehicle.

Speaking in excellent Polish, one of them began.

"You will join us and work as we have worked for nearly three weeks. You will be treated fairly and if things go right, we may even survive the war. This airbase is located somewhere south of Helu.

It was bombed by the German Luftwaffe at the very beginning of their invasion. We have been picked to rebuild the damage here, as much as possible, under limited Nazi enforcement."

"From what we hear, this is lucky duty. These German officers are quite liberal. They don't like being here anymore than we do. That is a good thing. They constantly talk of being home in Germany with their families. We can talk to them and receive favors that will keep us going."

He continued, "the food is not very good, but it is plentiful. You will not starve while you are here, we promise you that."

"We are a group of about twenty-five, and there are also about ten women and young girls who are here to clean and feed us. They too are prisoners and are being saved here with us. The women are all from Poland and many speak fluent German, as well."

"There are a dozen armed soldiers here, and several speak broken Polish. They too would rather be home in Germany with their friends and family."

"You will sleep with us in quarters once used by the Polish Air Force. The building is in reasonably descent shape. You will appreciate how clean and comfortable it is, compared to where you came from."

"This place was an airfield and was targeted by the Nazis just before their actual invasion. They completely destroyed the aircraft making it impossible for Polish retaliation from this field. Now the Nazis want to reuse this field for future air options. It may take us years to fully rebuild what they would want at this location."

"Maybe we could be here until the end of the war, whenever that may occur. Speaking of which, we have been told by a Polish farmer who brought milk to us that the war is not going well for Germany in many places. So, maybe things will change here as well. We don't really know."

"My name is Alberto. Please call me Al. These others are Klaus and Herbert. Please follow us to your bunk house and beds."

The three boys followed Al to the damaged Polish Air Force bunk garrison.

The door was a heavy structure and had bullet holes in the center. But inside was a bit of heaven for these three boys.

Al had been correct. The inside was amazingly clean and alive. There were pictures on the walls, flowers in the corners, and clean-looking bunk beds scattered throughout the large room.

A Nazi guard sat in a chair just to the right of the entrance. He smiled at the three boys, stood up, and said, "you may take any bed at the back on the left side."

Ivan, Hyman, and Felix quickly found comfortable beds. They stood by their beds speechless waiting for further directions.

Al finished talking to the guard and walked back to the boys' bed area. "If you want to, you guys can come with me to the kitchen for some food and drink."

"We are so hungry and appreciative," Hyman responded.

They followed Al out of the bunkhouse and walked to the kitchen building which was nearby.

They ate meat pies, potatoes, lemonade and milk. It was the best meal they had consumed since being taken by the Nazis.

There were smiles on the faces of the three boys. "Maybe God has found a way to save us," Hyman exclaimed.

CHAPTER ELEVEN

Their food was served by a middle-aged woman who had brought the food from the kitchen which was situated in the rear of the building.

She was the first woman they had seen since the train station many months earlier.

They noticed several other women working in the kitchen.

When they finished their meal, Al returned to take them to other areas of the base.

He quickly pointed out the battered condition of the airport runways and the collection of damaged aircraft piled up at the end of the tarmac.

At the beginning of the complex was a battered control tower which was being worked on by a number of prisoners.

Al told them that this area was a priority. "We all work there each day to eventually finish the rebuilding of this phase," he said.

"You will be working there with us starting tomorrow. Until then, you can go get some sleep and rest. Tomorrow will come soon enough."

The three boys walked back to their bunk house to attempt to catch-up on their much needed sleep.

CHAPTER TWELVE

The next morning, they enjoyed toasted brown bread with apple jelly and some butter served with terrible coffee and milk if one wanted it.

They were served by four young prisoner girls, dressed in prison clothing with their heads shaved, just like the rest in the room.

Ivan thought that each of the girls was attractive even in their present condition.

It was obvious that the girls had been allowed use of some basic cosmetics as their faces were clear and clean. No doubt they were very lucky to survive and be assigned to this airbase.

The boys were now among the labor force of the base and were brought to the control tower to join in the work.

A Nazi officer was in charge. He immediately approached these three new prisoners and spoke to them in broken Polish. "You will join the others in rebuilding this tower. Every two hours we will break and enjoy water and coffee. Please keep talking at a minimum."

Al walked behind Hyman and Felix and said, "Just pick up a brick and bring it to Ivan. He will be cementing bricks on this right side along with those other five. Remember, this is good work and you will not be in danger if we continue to show improvement to this tower and do other work for them."

Felix thanked him for the explanation and picked up his brick.

At noon they broke for lunch.

In the kitchen building they were met by the same young girls who were now setting the luncheon on the tables where they were about to sit.

In fluent Polish, one girl began to speak, "We are allowed to speak softly to you while continuing to work at our assignments. My name is Delora."

Ivan responded quickly, "Yes, we are all lucky to be here, Delora. My name is Ivan. I hope we can see each other often."

She brought him a meat and rice mix with a small scoops of carrot shavings on individual plates.

Waiting on the table were vats of milk and water.

After this limited luncheon, the girls brought homemade cookies to each table. The laborers were delighted even though the taste was not very good.

It was time to go back to work. But this time the guard marched them to the tower with smiles across their faces.

Brick by brick, the four sides of the tower began to rise.

Al had told them that they had spent nearly two weeks just cleaning up the debris that had formed around the broken tower.

And just two days ago, they had begun actually rebuilding the tower itself.

He also mentioned that there were other buildings that needed to be reconstructed not to mention the runway itself which was loaded with broken parts, holes, and even some bodies that had been killed during the German massacre.

"We have plenty of work ahead of us. Please think of it as a lucky stroke for our future."

CHAPTER THIRTEEN

On the second day, an airplane buzzed by. The guard recognized it as a Russian fighter. He expected that the German guns would shoot it down during its run.

The noise scared all of them. They had not heard much noise in this area for quite a while.

They went back to work building the tower, a little at a time.

At the next dinner they were served soup that had a spoiled taste to it. A large potato was sent along with it. Half an apple was given to each of them. Lemon drink and milk was available in quantity.

The same young girls served the food.

Delora spoke to Ivan upon his arrival in his seat. "You are new here. We haven't seen you before yesterday. Where are you from?"

"We three are from the Belarus area. What about you?"

"I am from an area south of Warsaw, but there is a girl here from Belarus that you should meet. I will send her to your table right after the meal."

The three boys ate what they wanted of the meal set before them.

When the meal time was over, Delora brought the Belarus girl to their table as promised.

"My God! Are you Brenda Cropsky?" Hyman screamed.

She answered in a soft returning voice, "Yes that is my name."

Ivan quickly asked, "What has happened to your face?"

"They forced me into sex with several officers and some of them beat me badly. I'm lucky I'm alive. And if it wasn't for a young German guard, I wouldn't be here today."

Hyman spoke, "Ivan and I both were very fond of you. We will now do what we can for you while we are here. Our stories are not much better. We are also lucky to be here with you and the others."

Al came up to their table and motioned for the boys to leave the building. The conversation with Brenda would have to wait until tomorrow.

Ivan and Hyman were shocked to find her here. "It must be God's wishes to have arranged this remarkable happening."

While walking away Ivan remarked, "Even without hair, a smashed face and an obvious state of depression, she still looks special to me."

"Yes, I would have to agree with you." Hyman returned.

CHAPTER
FOURTEEN

The bricks kept getting higher and the tower's brickwork program appeared to be coming to an end. The top floor, containing the control equipment and electrical power, would be completed later whenever the Nazis decided to order it done.

The prisoners were now directed to a building behind the kitchen building which was only partially destroyed in the bombing.

One side of the brick building took a bomb and it had not exploded.

Three volunteers had carefully taken the bomb out of the building and placed it on a platform truck.

The truck immediately drove off to another location to be detonated.

The prisoners were to rebuild that side with new bricks and mortar.

Al estimated it might take two weeks to complete the work.

The boys returned to their brick work similar to the tower program just completed.

Being located next to the kitchen building afforded Brenda the opportunity to converse more often with Ivan and Hyman each day.

On her way to kitchen duty and after kitchen duty, she would come close to the construction area and yell complementary words towards the boys.

It gave Hyman and Ivan something to look forward to each day.

They appreciated the attention and it was to help bring them closer to each other.

During the meals at the kitchen, they were very careful not to create attention that would be held against them.

They could still converse, but only in the course of serving the food and or cleaning the tables.

Brenda's hair began to grow back and the boys could see improvement in her battered facial bruises as well.

But they received word that an important Nazi officer was to arrive in two days and they were all to have their hair shaved before his arrival.

Even the boys' hair was beginning to reappear, but the base commandant wanted every prisoner to look as required by their leadership. So their looks quickly took a back spin for this approaching ceremony.

All the prisoners, the workers, the military guards, and the base officers stood at attention when the Nazi officer arrived.

He saluted the commandant and his staff. Then he walked through the lineup of prisoners and returned to face the whole group.

In loud German, he said, "I will now inspect what has been accomplished here. Then I must return to Berlin to report on several locations here in this part of Poland. Please lead me to your progress so I can report something good to the Fuhrer and the headquarters."

CHAPTER FIFTEEN

The Nazi officer was taken to the tower and he was shown pictures of before and after the repairs had been completed.

He appeared to be impressed and quickly returned to the group of awaiting prisoners.

The officer again walked among the formation of prisoners who were forced to stand at attention.

He looked at the back group of prison women. He stopped before them.

Speaking softly, he stated, "I can use a young woman now, and I will take this one with me." He pointed at Brenda Cropsky.

Two guards came forward and grabbed her by the arms and took her immediately to the officer's vehicle waiting at the entrance to the field.

He gave his final salute and stepped into the back seat with Brenda and motioned to the driver to leave.

Their vehicle sped off on the entrance road that had led them to the airfield.

Ivan and Hyman stood watching in horror.

CHAPTER SIXTEEN

Ivan spoke first.

"Her chance for survival is no longer good."

Hyman added, "Out of all the women, she was chosen. Why?"

Felix contributed, "She is still the most beautiful of all the girls. And he is a man. And most men choose beauty."

Ivan ended the discussion. "We should all pray for her."

Their commandant dismissed the group.

They all walked toward the kitchen building for lunch.

In about two weeks they had completed the restoration of the building behind the kitchen. Now new orders directed them to begin reconstruction of the runway itself.

The tarmac was in terrible shape, with holes throughout and parts of airplanes and even body pieces and bones were scattered along the whole length of the air strip.

Most of the large pieces and demolished aircraft were piled up at the very end of the lengthy field.

A truck was to be used to gather the loose items on the runway. All the prisoners were to help clear the way.

It would take several months to finally complete reconstruction reasonable enough before an aircraft would consider landing there.

By this time, the boys were nearly fourteen years-old.

Adolf Hitler had unwisely decided to attack the Soviet Union.

Although Hitler succeeded by conquering a great portion of Russia, the weather and poor preparedness stopped his army's advancement toward Moscow.

Britain and the United States began helping Russia fight the Nazis by supplying material, equipment, and weapons.

The Russian Army began a counter attack and was to beat the ill-prepared Nazis at every level.

It wasn't long before the largest invasion fleet ever to be assembled was being pieced together in rural England.

The invasion objective was to finally invade Hitler's possessions in Europe and to work their way toward Germany and to hopefully end the war.

By this time the Allies had begun eliminating the German Luftwaffe in the air and on their airfields obtaining control of the sky.

The timing of the Allies invasion was critical, and it finally began on the shores of Normandy, France on June 6th, 1944.

Within months, the Allies were re-conquering France city by city, and were poised to enter Germany.

The Russians were closing in on Germany from the other side and the end of the war seemed likely to happen soon.

Judicial General Fritz Gerhart was the officer who had visited the air strip where Ivan, Hyman, and Felix had been held prisoner.

He had been the one who handpicked Brenda Cropsky for his use. They had returned to Colon, Germany where he lived and was stationed.

He wore a pink Waffenfarbe on his uniform. It designated his control of the parked vehicles and equipment that was positioned in the greater- Colon area.

Although he was a married man with three children, he was to keep his Jewish mistress a secret.

He brought her to an apartment in nearby Konigswinter where he freely enjoyed her beauty with regular forced relations.

She did, however, receive good food and clothes and even cosmetics from him. But she was chained to a bedpost when he departed. He would leave food, water, and a large pan for her excretions within reach of her chain.

Bombing began taking place around the area as the war was coming closer. The Russians were nearly in Berlin and the Allies had crossed the Rhine River.

General Fritz had arranged for his family to leave immediately for Switzerland.

He was determined to stay the course. And he planned to enjoy his mistress as much as possible.

Only when the Allies entered Colon did he begin focusing on his personal concern.

As he did not want to be captured and feared the pain that could be put upon him, he realized that suicide might be the best way out.

He loaded his German Luger and decided to visit his mistress once more.

The general's conscience brought him to release the chains from Brenda's captivity and he actually thanked her for withstanding his personal demands upon her.

He told her that there would be deutsche marks in his wallet for her to use.

General Fitz put the gun to his head and pulled the trigger.

The noise brought individuals up from the apartment downstairs to discover Brenda.

They brought her with their family to a shelter built underground about a block away.

CHAPTER
SEVENTEEN

The first plane to arrive on the reconstructed airfield landed short of the runway, caught a bolder, and spun around and around. It lost a wheel and turned over at the edge of the patched tarmac.

The pilot was injured quite badly and his two passengers were bruised from head to toe. The plane was partially destroyed.

The two passengers had been sent from Berlin to deliver a letter from Reichsfuhrer Heinrich Himmler.

In the letter, Himmler demanded that there was to be no records or paper material left for the enemy. They were all to be burned.

The commandant received the letter from the injured passenger. He was asked to sign receipt of the document and it was to be filed by his assistant, who had been injured as well.

The passengers talked about the war which was about to be lost, and that the German military was being destroyed on most fronts.

They also believed that the Fuhrer and his staff would stay in Berlin under any circumstance to the very end.

These three injured men sought protection as well as medical help. Since there were no medical facilities, just kitchen supplies that had survived the bombing, only towels, soap, and aspirin were available.

The commandant offered his room near the entrance to the airfield for them to stay and said he would get a female prisoner to help with their recovery.

Delora was chosen to be the helper for the injured arrivals.

She told Felix that this could be good duty for her, getting her away from the kitchen duties and the other girls.

Delora had shown some interest in Felix over the past year since his arrival with Ivan and Hyman. The two complemented each other in many different ways.

There was space in the commandant's building for all three arrivals to sleep. An additional room that was partially burned-out was also available and could easily accommodate other beds.

Soldiers quickly cleared the area and brought a bed to the location.

Delora was asked to stay with them in the make-shift room.

The accommodation was not bad considering the situation.

She would continue changing towels and bring the limited supplies that were available from the kitchen to these injured arrivals.

Felix would see and talk to her at meal times.

A second plane came overhead, circled twice, released a parachuted parcel, and then left the area.

The chute landed on the tarmac about a hundred feet from the control tower.

Two guards raced to the parcel, untangled the chute, and brought the parcel to the awaiting officers and the commandant.

Within the parcel was a letter. The envelope was adorned with official Nazi insignias and was made of high-quality parchment.

The commandant began to open the imposing communication.

It was from the Fuhrer's official headquarters. It read:

> *"It has been determined that because of the condition of the war, all prisoners are to be eliminated as soon as possible before the arrival of the enemy. There are to be no exceptions, unless approved by the SS or our staff."*

The letter was signed by Reichfuhrer Honas Schwartzmizza, assistant to the Fuhrer, with the stamped insignia of the Third Reich boldly displayed at the bottom.

The commandant was in a state of shock.

He rolled up the letter and put it in an inside pocket of his uniform.

In German, he announced to his awaiting soldiers that it appeared the war may be over soon. But the Fuhrer's people were demanding unreasonable conditions.

"We will wait until our capture and face the reality of defeat. We will not make any changes here, under my command."

CHAPTER EIGHTEEN

The bombing continued around Colon and Konigswinter. Brenda was well cared for in the safe underground tunnel.

Available food included brown bread, soup, sausages, and some fruit.

The family that had taken her to this safe-haven was very friendly and concerned about her.

Her face was still in rough shape, but her hair was just starting to grow again, and she was still dressed in worn and dirty prisoner clothes.

The other people in the tunnel did not look very favorable toward that family or Brenda.

They sat against the wooden planks that were supporting the tunnel. No benches or other furniture was inside.

This group of about thirty individuals stayed together and slept against the wooden supports, on and off, for 24 hours.

Finally, the bombing stopped and they began to leave the tunnel.

What they didn't know was that the final bombing of the war had taken place in their section of the Rhine River.

The British and U.S. advancing troops had made their way towards Colon.

They had captured Bonn and were within the limits of Konigswinter. Colon was but a few hours away.

Brenda was taken back to the residence below the place that she had been held captive.

The family gave her a bed and some clothes. She was able to wash and be clean for the first time in weeks.

Although she could not converse in German to thank them, she found a way to do so in her native Polish language.

They had recognized since the day of the General's suicide that she had been treated badly and that she was a Jew.

But now the German soldiers were no longer on the streets.

Two buildings next to their resident building had been demolished by the last bombing raid. A woman lay dead next to one of the doorsteps.

A tank was coming up the hill on a torn-up road from the south. Following it were two vehicles carrying troops.

Upon close examination, they could see they were Allied forces overtaking what was left of German defenses along the road.

The British and American flags were waving brightly from the vehicles.

Resistance was tight, and the war appeared to be over.

CHAPTER
NINETEEN

Two British aircraft landed on the reconstructed tarmac near where Ivan, Hyman,
and Felix were being held captive.

Six British Lancers came off the first aircraft
quickly. They were equipped with rifles and were
dressed in fighting uniforms.

The commandant and his men were stood at attention with their hands in the air.

In broken English, the commandant spoke, "We surrender without condition. We have taken excellent care of the prisoners who had been assigned to this location and hereby request leniency in our treatment."

The British lieutenant responded at once. "If what you say is true, we will see what we can do for you. Please put down your hands and lay your weapons on the ground at once."

They dropped their belts, revolvers, and other weapons to the pavement, as requested.

Two of the Lancers ran into the kitchen building to investigate.

Coming off the second plane were six more soldiers who immediately began to search the outer areas of the field.

The war had finally ended at this Polish location.

The Russians were to claim this territory and much more.

All the prisoners welcomed the British soldiers, the girls with hugs and the boys with firm hand-shakes.

The girls had even baked cookies for such an occasion.

All the soldiers and prisoners enjoyed this special celebration.

Milk was still plentiful and fresh lemonade was poured to quench everyone's thirst.

But all of them wondered, what will happen next?

CHAPTER TWENTY

The family took Brenda to the town hall in Konigswinter. It had been bombed and the back side of the brick building was damaged. The front of the edifice was still in reasonably decent shape.

A large sign with a swastika lay at the dirt entrance, with half of it covered with bullet holes.

Upon entering they noticed a paper sign hanging in front of them hand-written in bold German, "Of local interest to the left, and all others to the right."

There were two broken desks in the room with three official-looking individuals behind each desk.

Six people were in front of them. They were forced to wait their turn.

Brenda's temporary family members waited with her.

They were finally called to the desk on the right.

In excellent German, the family attempted to explain Brenda's situation to the officials.

"We cannot move her back to Poland at this time. Maybe in several weeks when transportation is returned and the government approves her movement," stated the chief official.

"Meanwhile, stay close and continue to check with us each week," he finished.

"Next please!" he yelled.

The family assured Brenda that she could remain with them until they found a way to return her to Poland.

Brenda understood the situation and hugged members of the family.

They started back toward the family residence.

While walking, they saw total destruction of buildings, vehicles, and equipment of all kinds, some lying in the center of the beat-up roads and others pushed or blown to the sides of the streets.

People seemed to be everywhere. Some were looking for lost individuals while others were trying to make some sort of acceptance of their future lives.

The visual results of the war in Germany seemed to be total destruction in all directions.

Brenda now realized how lucky she had been to have been discovered by this caring family.

She reached into her pocket and produced two hundred deutsche marks which she had taken from her rapist's pocket.

"Please take these marks," she responded in Polish as she put them into the hands of the family's mother.

She graciously accepted the currency.

CHAPTER
TWENTY-ONE

The British commandos had taken over the airfield. They did not have to fight anyone or change anything that had been happening at this location.

British intelligence told them to hold the airfield until the Russians arrived. They estimated it would be within the next week or perhaps sooner.

The prisoners were celebrating their survival, having received information that the British would see to it that all the prisoners would be helped to return to their home areas as soon as possible.

Dealing with the Russians was not a concern at this time.

There was no more construction work for the prisoners. They were told to rest and prepare for their eventual movement.

Delora and Felix used this time to really get to know each other.

They soon became lovers.

They realized that they had experienced much together and that their attraction to each other was important. They began to plan their future together.

Ivan and Hyman applauded the couple and their outward commitment to each other.

The rest of the prisoners also gave their approval.

Two of the British officers who spoke broken Polish offered to transport Delora and Felix anywhere they wanted to go to begin their new life together.

Felix responded, "England, please England!"

One of the officers replied, "We can do that for you, we promise."

Delora and Felix now had their hopes for a new life promised to them.

Four days later the Russians arrived.

One of the Russian officers spoke fluent English. He had been educated in Britain eight years before.

"We have been assured that all of Poland belongs now to us. We are to restore the area and have authority to transport prisoners back to their home areas. It may take several more days before transportation can be available. We are camped outside your field and do not need anything at this time. We will return to seek information from your prisoners to learn where they are to be transported. Please keep everything in order, for now."

They saluted the British officers and left the airfield.

CHAPTER TWENTY-TWO

Nearly a month had gone bye when Brenda's family was told that the town official had located a Polish organization that would consider taking surviving Jews to a Polish processing center to be evaluated for a potential settlement appointment.

A woman had followed her home to interpret those words into the Polish language so that

Brenda could understand what they wanted to do with her.

She was also told that Poland had been taken over entirely by the Russians and that communism would rule the country.

"No!" she said to the interpreter. "I don't want my life controlled by the Russians. I want to go elsewhere, maybe to Spain or England. Please tell them and let me know as soon as possible," she answered.

Brenda told the interpreter that she had lost her family, her mother, and her father who was shot and killed in her house.

Also, her two brothers had left several weeks earlier for the United States via boat from free Spain.

There would be no reason to go back to Poland.

She asked the interpreter to please tell the family of her situation.

The interpreter immediately told the waiting family standing behind her.

Two members of the family came forward to hug her.

Spain was in battered condition. The Nazis had demolished many of the cities and a revolution within the country had favored possible communist control.

England was the better choice and the closest for independence and freedom.

Fortunately, the British were in the area still helping to clear the debris that had made the streets of Germany immoveable.

One of the city officials stopped a British officer and in broken English told him of Brenda's request.

He agreed to help her go to England.

"Please get her ready. I will be back to get her to-morrow. I will arrange a flight for her. We are flying out of a damaged base not far up the Rhine."

The news was immediately brought to Brenda.

She was delighted.

"I can't believe that they will get me this chance to begin a new life in a free country. Wow, I will be ready." She was elated and had tears in her eyes.

CHAPTER TWENTY-THREE

Felix and Delora squeezed into a small British airplane that was already stuffed with equipment.

The pilot was a young officer who welcomed them in the only language he knew, which of course was proper English.

They figured it out and responded in Polish that they were happy to be on his airplane.

The aircraft moved down the runway and made its way into the sky.

Approximately two hours later they landed in Birmingham, England.

The tarmac and the airport buildings were loaded with military personnel, and equipment was strewn in every direction.

The pilot brought them into a crowded office at the end of the terminal building.

A high-ranking officer had them sign a form with their names printed as best as they could.

The officer picked up a telephone and spoke quickly.

"Please wait," he stated. "Take a seat."

Within minutes, a well-dressed military woman appeared who spoke fluent Polish, "We are prepared to give you a new start. It will begin tomorrow morning. For now, you will be taken to an army hospital for medical inspection and you will sleep there tonight. Welcome to Great Britain. We hope that you are well enough to begin to enjoy our wonderful country, with us. All your questions will be answered tomorrow. I will be there with you."

The happy young couple walked out to a waiting car to take them to the Army hospital for their first night of real freedom.

CHAPTER TWENTY-FOUR

The Russian officer returned and announced, "we will soon take you Jews back to Warsaw to help rebuild the city."

"I am not a Jew," responded Ivan. "I am Catholic and not one of them."

"But you have been processed and labored as a Jew, yes?" the officer countered.

"Yes, but I am not a Jew and should not have been taken and treated as a Jew," Ivan insisted.

"Well then, we will not be taking you back to Warsaw. They only want Jews," the officer stated. "We shall send you to another area. Would you want to go to Russia, with us?"

"No, I want to go to America or England," Ivan demanded.

"If I can find someone to take you, then fine. Please give me some time." The officer turned his back to Ivan and walked toward the kitchen.

Hyman grabbed Ivan by the arm and said, "I will go back to Warsaw and will seek relatives and friends that might have survived. I will try to make a new life there. I cannot go with you. Maybe they can help me with my eye that was destroyed. It is my best bet. My Jewish heritage must survive as well. They have not taken away my pride... of being a Jew. I know that you will do well wherever you end up. We will try to keep in touch no matter."

Ivan nodded his head, and the two of them began moving toward the kitchen building.

Russian aircraft began to land at the airfield. Several brought food and supplies for the kitchen building and for the increased numbers who were arriving by plane and in other vehicles.

A small Dutch aircraft landed the very next day delivering two Russian immigrants who had been held prisoner in a nearby town by the Nazis.

The Russian officer greeted the plane and welcomed the released prisoners coming off the aircraft.

He stopped the pilot and asked him if he could take a released prisoner back with him to Holland.

He replied, "I am heading for Paris, then London. I am bringing documents and mail to government officials. But if there is only one passenger, I can take him."

And with that, Ivan was headed out of Poland. He was thrilled at the chance to leave the Nazi compound. That night, the remaining prisoners held a going away party for Ivan.

They gave him a piece of the red brick that he worked with for most of his time there. It was wrapped in soft cloth and put into a sleeve that came from the building supplies.

He told them that he would always treasure it, not because of what it meant, but because it represented all of individuals with whom he shared these forced labors.

Ivan was awakened at early dawn and told to pack what his personal items and hurry to the south end of the tarmac. With a small bag of cookies, brown bread, and the piece of red brick, he mounted the steps to the Dutch aircraft.

Several hours later they landed at an airport just west of Paris.

They were met by a French soldier who was waiting for documents and mail.

The pilot and the soldier spoke in French. They laughed and shook hands.

Within minutes the plane took off toward London.

CHAPTER TWENTY-FIVE

Three days later, Russian trucks arrived to transport the remaining prisoners back to Warsaw.

The prisoners were concerned where the Russians might take them.

The Russian official at the base could not answer their questions.

He told them that others made decisions the as to where or when, and that they would not have a choice of anything at this stage.

The Russians were to make them help rebuild the city of Warsaw.

Hyman requested medical help for his eye.

They claimed that there were not any medical facilities available at that time.

Four months later they took him to a field hospital and he was examined.

Unfortunately, there was nothing they could do for him. He was told that he would have to live without sight in that eye for the rest of his life.

Hyman was trained to be a carpenter and worked diligently at his job helping to rebuild several of the edifices that had been destroyed during the war.

He joined the union and became an advisor. Later he was forced to join the communist party.

Along the way he met a woman named Beatrice who was ten years older than him. They would marry.

CHAPTER TWENTY-SIX

The Dutch aircraft landed safely on a makeshift airfield on the outskirts of London. The airstrip was at a large factory that had produced candles and kitchen items before the war.

A Luftwaffe bomb had destroyed the factory. The parking area had now become the landing strip.

The military was now calling it an airfield. Two British planes were parked at the very end of the strip.

The Dutch pilot taxied the craft to a small shed located near the British planes at the end of the runway.

The pilot opened his door and dropped to the ground then came around the plane to help Ivan depart the aircraft.

"Welcome to freedom," the pilot blurted.

"Thank God." Ivan responded in broken English.

He bent over and kissed the tarmac.

A British soldier came out of the shed to greet them.

After the pilot explained Ivan's situation to an officer, they sent him to official headquarters several blocks away.

There, after a hot shower, he was given fresh military clothes to wear.

Next they brought him to a room filled with local volunteers.

The volunteers were assigned to help lost people, to find missing individuals affected by the war, and to help in the settlement of those who were in need of housing.

An interpreter came forward to help Ivan with his needs.

His mind turned immediately towards attempting to locate Brenda even though she was last known to have been taken to Germany.

The interpreter told him that locating someone in Germany would have to be dealt with at another building in downtown London.

After hearing of Ivan's background, he was sent to a boarding house arranged and paid for by the British government.

He was given a pleasant room and was told to get some sleep.

But first he was afforded an excellent luncheon prepared by the house family.

He enjoyed eggs, ham, and muffins with real coffee.

His stomach was full for the first time since he had been home in Belarus.

Now he was ready for a good sleep.

CHAPTER TWENTY-SEVEN

Felix and Delora were given three months free rent in a furnished apartment just outside Birmingham, England.

They were now nearly twenty years old, so grateful to be alive, and grateful to be together.

Their hair had finally grown back and now they looked like the other British citizens around them.

Both had picked-up reasonable amounts of the English language and proudly speak to each other in the language each day.

Felix was working as a counselor at a British scout camp.

Delora walked daily about a mile to a school to train to become a cook.

After she completes her six months of schooling, she will be assigned to a job using her newly developed skills.

They were very much in love and were considering marriage during the next year.

Felix tried to locate Ivan, Hyman, and even Brenda without success.

Delora was attempting to locate some of her relatives who were displaced during the same period as her abduction.

She was praying that some of her family might have survived.

Unfortunately, the channels for finding individuals, quality communications, and international cooperation that was vitally needed had just begun, and millions of people were desperately seeking their loved ones, just as they were.

By 1948 the program seemed to be working quite well.

Felix and Delora joined a Polish displacement organization in London and went to their meetings each month.

Many of the membership came from Warsaw and two came from Belarus.

They meet to help each other in the settlement adjustments that are required in their new country.

Three of the members were disabled and needed many favors and special help.

All of the members were made homeless by the war and were so grateful to be in this free and safe country.

CHAPTER TWENTY-EIGHT

Ivan was happy with his boarding house that had been arranged and paid for by the British government. Soon a government agency located a part-time job for him in a rehabilitation center on the other side of London.

Although the pay was not so good, he was able to save some of the sterling that he earned.

Ivan often thought of Brenda, Hyman, Felix, and Delora. But his major concern was to locate Brenda.

Finally, he was able to visit the other military building that was recommended to him at the processing center They investigated internationally lost individuals.

They listed Ivan on the "seeking" list and could not do any more for him at that time.

In his job at the rehabilitation center, he was able to learn English and with it made several new friendships.

Among this group of new friends was a very pretty young lady named Elizabeth. She was a couple of years older than Ivan.

Elizabeth began to appreciate Ivan's attempt to share his background with her and the others.

Ivan, in broken English, told of his father's murder, his mother and sister's captivity, and the fact that he did not know if they had survived.

Elizabeth volunteered to help him get answers.

As a favor, she would visit the research buildings and report to him regularly. He couldn't help becoming fond of her.

They would meet after work in a small pub near the exit of their employ.

They enjoyed a small beer together, reviewing any and all information that had been gathered during the time they had been apart.

Elizabeth lived in a suburb of London with her elderly mother. Her father had perished in a fire following a bombing in a building just two blocks from her home.

Her family had cursed the Nazis for the bombing and the loss of her father.

Ivan was invited to dinner at her house one day after work.

He followed Elizabeth into the tunnel and took the working trolley to her suburb stop.

Ivan purchased some basic flowers to bring with him from a beckoning young boy in the bowels of the subway.

Elizabeth was impressed.

He gave the flowers to her mother immediately upon entering their warm and gracious home.

Her elderly mother hadn't received anything since before the war and was overwhelmed by the gesture.

Elizabeth and her mother were taken by his thoughtfulness and charm.

When Ivan said his goodbyes, Elizabeth gently kissed him on the lips.

It was the beginning of a romance needed by both of them.

They became inseparable.

The lack of social contact between the sexes during wartime was evident among the survivors.

The obvious priority during that period was to win the conflict at any cost.

Social contact took a backseat in most individual's lives.

Ivan and Elizabeth, both quite young, were built up with emotional needs that needed to be addressed.

Elizabeth was invited to see Ivan's room at the boarding house.

There, they were to make love like few ever do.

They tore each other apart, enjoying the needed emotional lift that lovers ultimately discover.

Their intercourse shook the foundation of the building.

She was in love. Ivan was not sure.

Elizabeth kept visiting the research buildings hoping to find Ivan's important information.

She had hopes of maybe ending his concern for his family and friends.

Elizabeth also had hopes of a future marriage.

CHAPTER TWENTY-NINE

Hyman continued to work in the rebuilding of Warsaw. He was told that his work was not satisfactory, and he became outraged.

His wife was bitter and unhappy with her life.

The communist party demanded money from them as well as more productivity from their work.

His wife was a volunteer at the local hospital along with many other survivors.

Hyman visited the local communist headquarters and expressed his dissatisfaction at his inability to meet their requirements.

They warned him to complete their demands or risk being sent to their camps in Siberia.

After a long discouraging talk with his wife, he committed suicide.

His wife is sent to Siberia.

Many years later, when Poland is finally freed of the communists, the surviving Jewish community erected a statue of Hyman Goldenstein–his stone would tell the story of his life, as a Jew.

CHAPTER THIRTY

Many months earlier, Brenda left Colon, Germany via a British airplane and landed in a suburb of London.

She had been assigned to a Polish relief group that formed at the time.

Her luck had changed, and she was taken in by a Polish-English family near the City of

Birmingham. Their family had lost a daughter in the war who had been serving in the British military at Warsaw when the conflict began.

And so Brenda, their house guest, immediately was given the daughter's room and clothes.

Brenda was helped by the mother who spoke fluent Polish, "please enjoy our late daughter's position in our family. We are pleased to have someone even attempting to take her place in our home."

"I am overwhelmed. I will do whatever I can to show my appreciation for your kindness," Brenda responded.

Soon she became a British-looking free young woman.

She could not believe how lucky she had become in this new country. The family's hospitality was truly remarkable.

Brenda's beautiful hair had grown back, and her face had healed to the point that some of the late daughter's makeup disguised the imperfections that she had received in captivity.

The new family recognized the change in Brenda's appearance and attitude. She had gained back her confidence.

But Brenda worried about the survival of her family, relatives, and friends.

And she would often turn her thoughts to Ivan and Hyman, and of course Felix and Delora.

Brenda did not know where to begin investigating their whereabouts.

She decided to ask her new family if they could help.

The father of the family, although quite elderly, offered his connections to the British military for a chance to check the international seek list that might be available.

And so, a phone call to the military authorities produced some hope. No promises were assured.

Meanwhile Brenda worked around the house cleaning all the rooms, sweeping the floors, and planting flowers and vegetables.

This family quickly adored her for her personality, appreciation, and household contributions that she continued to make.

One day the doorbell rang and a young soldier stood there with an envelope in his hand.

It was addressed to Brenda Cropsky from the war office in London.

They had located some of the information that she requested.

It read, "We have been informed that your family name has been eliminated in Balara. There is no word or information about any other family names or locations. We are continuing our search for the whereabouts of your friends and associates. Thank you for your patience and co-operation on this matter."

Signed Reginald P. Plympton, CC, British Lanciers

CHAPTER
THIRTY-ONE

Elizabeth recieved a message from the British Intelligence Office that they had located the name Brenda Cropsky in Konigswinter, Germany.

No further information had been received.

Elizabeth immediately reported the finding to her boyfriend Ivan.

"I must go to Germany to find her. Hopefully she has survived," he replied.

"I will leave tomorrow somehow. Please don't stop me. I will return as soon as possible."

The next morning Ivan left his boarding house with a small bag over his shoulder and walked to the nearest underground subway.

He got off the transportation at a stop reading, "British Airforce Base."

Ivan walked several blocks to the entrance to the base.

He explained his situation to a soldier at the gate.

The soldier offered to guide him to the proper office.

There, the military graciously accepted him on a flight to Bonn, Germany, which was the closest to Colon that the British could fly at the time.

And so Ivan boarded this cargo plane headed for Germany.

He was told that Bonn was not far from Konigswinter and Colon.

After a very bumpy landing, he arrived on a heavily destroyed air strip.

Ivan, with no knowledge of the German language, began hitchhiking on a major road a few blocks away from the landing location.

A German Volkswagen stopped ahead of him.

A German soldier jumped out of the front seat and waved him into his vehicle.

The driver was headed toward Colon and would attempt leaving him in Konigswinter if the roads were cleared from the war debris.

They soon found out that the roads were not cleared enough for vehicles to pass at that time.

And so, Ivan had no choice but to go on to Colon.

He spent several nights there attempting to find out whether the roads were to be clear if he made another try to get through to the center of Konigswinter.

Finally, a Dutch doctor was located who was preparing to go to Konigswinter and other cities in the general area.

He agreed to take Ivan with him the following week.

Ivan was determined to find Brenda, no matter what it took.

He remembered his fondness for her, her beauty, and her special personality.

This remembrance helped keep his focus to find her.

CHAPTER
THIRTY-TWO

Brenda received a second letter ten days later. This letter acknowledged that they had found that an Ivan Kanofsky had entered Germany.

It further stated that British officials in Germany would attempt to personally locate him, tell him of the request, and communicate with him directly.

The letter caught Brenda by surprise.

She thought that Ivan might try to find her in Germany and hoped someone would tell him of her movement to England.

"I knew, if he survived, he would attempt to find me. It is wonderful that he is alive. If things go right, we will meet again maybe soon," she blurted in excitement.

Her family knew how meaningful this letter had been for Brenda. They encouraged her to thank God.

Brenda quickly placed her hands together and propped her head towards the ceiling and responded in broken English, "Thank you, God."

She then told the family members of her need to find the others who had been with her during their captivity, namely Hyman, Felix, and Delora.

"Maybe Ivan might know of their whereabouts. I'm sure he will be as concerned as I am now," she continued.

Brenda slept well that night. She dreamed about seeing Ivan and the others again.

CHAPTER
THIRTY-THREE

The doctor did what he had promised and drove Ivan to Konigswinter. Then Ivan thanked him.

The doctor responded, "You Jews don't have to thank me."

Ivan responded, "I am not a Jew. I am Catholic and have been falsely treated as a Jew. But I thank you for what you have done for me, and not because you thought I was a Jew."

In Konigswinter, he walked around the city center which had been bombed quite badly.

He noticed several people with shaved heads and decided to stop a couple walking side by side.

"Do you speak Polish?" he asked.

"Yes, we are from Warsaw and have by some miracle survived the camp. These German officials will help you find your loved ones, if they have survived. Just go two more blocks in that direction and you will see a large sign for 'Seekers.'"

In Hebrew, they said, "We wish you much luck. Shalom."

Ivan walked the several blocks to the "Seekers" sign. It was mounted on a smashed German tank which stood in front of a bombed-out school.

There in the street were tables and chairs set-up to help refugees and lost individuals. The line had two columns.

Ivan quickly joined a line. He was at the very end of the group before him.

Nearly two hours later he reached the front of the line and began talking to an interpreter who spoke broken Polish.

Upon hearing his name, they sent him to another table which was set up just for Jews.

When he realized that it was for Jews only, he explained that he was not a Jew, but had been treated as one.

He quickly found out that the table was to help transport Polish Jews back to Poland.

So, Ivan went back to the original table and told of his problem.

They referred him to a building several blocks in another direction. There he was to meet British and American representatives who were just settling into a battered building. They had a makeshift sign written in chalk that said, "International Help."

Only two individuals waited ahead of him when he arrived.

One individual was wrapped in bandages and had a cane.

The other was a young man and was missing an arm.

Anxiously, Ivan waited for his turn.

CHAPTER
THIRTY-FOUR

Brenda waited anxiously for additional information. She wouldn't leave the house. Her usual chores were done routinely as her mind was continuing to focus on the hopeful survival of her friends.

A week went by and finally another letter arrived.

It indicated that Ivan had been located by British officials in Konigswinter, Germany.

The letter said that he had been looking for Brenda for several weeks, finally locating the family that helped her, and living below the apartment where she was held hostage.

He had been told that she had tried to go to England or maybe even America, but they were not sure.

It said Ivan assured officials he would accept a military ride to greater London when one would become available. The case was number 19003.

Brenda was jubilant and hugged two of her family members.

She now knew, for sure, that Ivan had discovered that she was alive and that she could probably be somewhere in London or America.

"I will put my name and your address in the London newspaper and in the Polish paper as well in hopes that he will find it soon. And if he has gone to America, I must find out and see what to do next. My contact in the military will surely help me," she said.

Several weeks were to go by before anything was to happen.

Brenda went to church with her adopted family on Sunday morning, where she prayed for the survival of her family and friends.

When they arrived home, there was a note attached to the front door.

It was hand written in Polish.

"My name is Elizabeth. I live in Birmingham where Ivan has been staying prior to leaving for Germany to hopefully find you and the others. The local Polish newspaper had listed many Polish individuals looking for each other. I found your name and temporary address on the listing. Ivan told me your name and so it connected with me right away. He will surely come back to my residence when he returns. I will tell him of our communication. No doubt he will want to come to meet you. I detect his fondness for you."

The note was signed, "Elizabeth."

Brenda began crying, "He will come here, for sure."

CHAPTER
THIRTY-FIVE

Brenda washed her hair and chose a pretty paisley skirt and white blouse to wear. The family mother bought her a pair of black shoes in her size. The shoes that belonged to their late daughter did not fit Brenda.

Her mood was the best it had been since her days back home in Poland with her own family.

It had been nine days since Elizabeth's letter and Brenda was beginning to wonder if Ivan had run into problems getting to England.

She had no address for Elizabeth and knew that she and she alone must bring Ivan to her. "I don't even know her last name, only that she lives in Birmingham."

Meanwhile, Felix and Delora had read the same Polish paper and discovered Brenda's address in it as well.

Felix was readying to go to Brenda's address. Delora was not feeling well and opted to stay at their residence.

He arranged for a taxi to take him to the address.

Felix now had a full head of hair and had put on about thirty pounds since being a prisoner.

His minimal income afforded him the opportunity to purchase some colorful clothing from a local department store that had survived the war.

He wondered what Brenda and the others would look like since he last saw them.

The taxi approached the house.

Felix paid the driver and the taxi left the area.

He walked to the front door of the simple English cottage.

The doorbell had been disconnected during the war, saving on electricity and money. It had not yet been reconnected.

Felix knocked on the door with both hands.

The woman of the family came to open it.

She greeted him with a smile and in English said, "Please come in."

"I am Felix and have come to meet Brenda," he responded.

"Please wait here. I will tell her of your arrival."

Brenda thought the commotion at the door was Ivan arriving.

When she came in from the backyard where she had been watering the plants and vegetables, she was frightened to see a man waiting in the front entrance she did not recognize.

"What has happened to Ivan?" she yelled.

"I am Felix, remember me? he immediately responded. "I don't know anything about Ivan. But, how are you?"

"Wow. I'm sorry. I didn't recognize you. You have changed, and for the better! But I was expecting Ivan." Brenda responded.

"Is he really coming here?" Felix returned.

"Yes, he has been in Germany looking for me. Thankfully the British government located him, and he has found me. Maybe he will arrive while you are here. Please sit down and tell me about you and Delora."

Felix did relax on a couch in the living room where he began to explain his and Delora's survival to Brenda.

The family mother brought tea and homemade cookies to them in the living room.

One hour later there was a knock on the front door.

Brenda jumped up and ran to the entrance.

There, standing on the front steps, was Ivan with a woman.

He was dressed in a military uniform that had been given to him upon landing in London. His other clothing had become a mess. He had been living in those clothes for many days.

His hair, which had grown back, was neatly combed and his face was clear and clean. He carried a pleasant smile as he addressed Brenda. Listening in the background was Felix.

"Your beauty is more than intact. I have waited for this happening since being forced to leave you and our friends many moons ago. This is my friend Elizabeth," he blurted.

CHAPTER THIRTY-SIX

Delora was sick. She knew it and kept as much as she could from Felix. A doctor's appointment at the local clinic tomorrow would tell her what could be wrong.

Felix had returned from his special meeting with Ivan, Brenda and Elizabeth.

He was thrilled by the successful celebration that had taken place.

Delora finally told him of her pain, and that an appointment had been made for tomorrow at the clinic.

Her doctor announced that she had advanced pulmonary disease and that her future was very doubtful.

Medical knowledge during that period was limited. Guesswork was a regular answer from inexperienced doctors.

He gave her medicine to take to help with the pain only.

Three days later Delora passed away at home… in the arms of Felix.

Their friends found the way to Felix's house in Birmingham. Elizabeth had picked flowers from her backyard and brought a bunch for Felix.

Felix was taken by her gift because she hardly knew him and had not met Delora at all.

They each gave him sympathy and personal hugs.

Delora was cremated and her ashes were to be kept by Felix.

Ivan, Brenda, and Elizabeth vowed to keep in touch with Felix as they left his home in Birmingham.

A few days later, Ivan returned to visit Brenda.

He explained his association with Elizabeth to her as only a friend who had helped him pull together when he arrived in Britain.

"She knew from the beginning that I needed to find you, Brenda, and the others, and that my personal feelings were really for you. Although she wanted more from me, I made it quite clear that my hopes were for your survival and for my affection toward you. She totally understands, and being the great person that she is, has been very happy for me and for you now that we have met once again," he stated.

"I'm overwhelmed by your story. I need someone like you in my life. Since the first day I met you when I was a young girl, I thought you were possibly the type of person that I could make a life with," she responded.

Ivan moved closer and met her lips. She began to cry, "I know that I love you, Ivan. I'm very lucky and happy," she continued.

"We must get together. I cannot be away from you very much longer. I am in love with you and we must be together as soon as possible," Ivan responded.

They kissed again and again.

Finally he said, "Goodbye for now. You will hear from me tomorrow. Remember, I love you."

Two days later, Brenda discovered in the Polish newspaper that Hyman Goldenstein had committed suicide in Warsaw.

He had been buried in a family plot near Belarus. He left a pregnant wife, Julliette.

Brenda immediately notified Ivan and Felix. They were all in shock at his passing and by the means that he chose.

He had been a dear friend, and like Ivan, had adored Brenda both in their early years and throughout their prison captivity.

And although he was a Jew like Brenda, she tended to favor Ivan even if he was not a Jew, just treated as one.

But they all had good relationship with Hyman. He was truly one of the gang and would be missed.

Their feelings of sympathy were for Hyman's widow Juliette who none of them had ever met.

They had no way to contact her directly but agreed to attempt to do so in the future.

CHAPTER
THIRTY-SEVEN

Three months later, Ivan and Brenda followed Felix into a furnished apartment just outside Birmingham, England, with three months free rent.

They were now a close threesome.

Ivan had taken a job in the construction industry helping to rebuild parts of London that had been destroyed by the Nazis during the war.

He actually returned to a position similar to what he worked in the prison camp, taking bricks and cementing them.

They gave him this job because of his experience of having done it before. The pay was quite good, and it afforded him a decent living at that time.

Brenda began working at a brewery doing administrative services and serving as an interpreter for Polish communications.

Elizabeth maintained a relationship with Felix. They had become an item.

Both had taken work with the government, holding positions of importance with the government's dealings with Polish immigrants.

Their pay was increasing each month and they were happy at their jobs.

The four of them would meet each Sunday for breakfast.

Ivan had researched life in the United States.

The media in England continued to speak and write about the heroic effort they had received from America–both Canada and United States– during their most destitute moments in World War II.

Prime Minister Winston Churchill spoke regularly about the special people of the United States and their support and sacrifice on Britain's behalf during those terrible years.

"We shall never be able to repay them for what they did for us," he remarked.

Ivan thought that America might be better for them as England had become very crowded with immigrants and alike after the war.

One day he noticed an advertisement in the local London newspaper that construction workers and general laborers were needed In New York. One half the transportation to reach the United States would be paid by the company, to those who qualify.

He immediately applied for the job, highlighting his background and learned skills in the construction industry.

Two days later they hired him, in writing, and authorized him to come to America as soon as possible.

The pay was to be a major increase over what he was presently being given. He was elated, to say the least.

"Let's go!" he told Brenda. "We can get married either here or there, wherever you would like," he continued.

Brenda was overwhelmed. She took two deep breaths and replied, "I would love to marry you Ivan, but we should do it here with our friends," she responded.

And so, Brenda and Ivan were to plan a small but beautiful wedding in a hurry so that they could leave for America in about four days.

Felix volunteered to be the best man and Elizabeth offered to serve Brenda in any way she would like.

Brenda's temporary family offered to have the event in their living room. She thought the offer was terrific and committed to that location at once.

Ivan was not a Jew but would accept a justice to perform the ceremony in both Polish and English.

The Polish newspaper located a justice who could do it in both languages.

The wedding date was to be in two days, at twelve noon.

Ivan teased Felix, "Why don't you marry Elizabeth and come along with us to America? We would help you find work there, and you two could live with us until you could afford to get your own residence."

Felix responded, "Don't laugh. I'll run it by Elizabeth."

CHAPTER THIRTY-EIGHT

Felix got down on his knees in front of Elizabeth. "Will you marry me and come with me, Ivan, and Brenda to America?"

She responded immediately, "You must be kidding! Yes!"

"We could get married with them in two days and leave with them on the fourth day," he answered.

Elizabeth phoned her mother and sister. They were excited and would attend the event with pleasure.

Felix ran down the hall to tell Ivan and Brenda.

Brenda yelled, "We will gladly share our special day with you love birds."

The wedding day arrived, and light snow graced the ground around the family house, the location for the dual weddings.

Reverend Dr. James Sikorsky prepared the ceremony. He had been a chaplain in the Polish Army but had retired and moved to England with his English wife prior to the beginning of the war.

Reverend James reminded all the participants how lucky they all were to have come through that long and terrible Second World War.

In Polish, he thanked God for allowing this day to happen.

He also thanked the host family for the use of their lovely home for the event.

His quick ceremony, in the presence of God, was bestowed upon both couples in broken English.

Both grooms kissed their brides, and then exchanged kisses as well.

Hugs were given to everyone by the family members of the house and by Elizabeth's mother and sister.

Polish sausages and English fish and chips were prepared for the wedding dinner. Scones and muffins were supplemented by wine and apple juices.

It was a lovely setting and a small but beautiful layer cake followed served by the hostess.

The Reverend James made a toast to the happiness of both couples in their marriages.

Several months earlier, no one would have believed this event possible.

CHAPTER
THIRTY-NINE

Hyman's widow Juliette received a long letter from Brenda. Brenda chose to introduce the group that never had the chance to meet her.

She mentioned each name and some background that included her late husband Hyman.

In Polish, she told of her fondness for him and the others, and how they vowed to stay together as long as possible.

Brenda told her how Hyman was forced to go back to Poland and that he had hoped to live a new life.

She said that they had heard that he had married you and that the rest of the group thought he had begun a happy new life.

Within the news of his passing it was mentioned that you were pregnant.

With the birth of a child possible, the group would hope his or her name could carry Hyman's in the child's naming.

Brenda mentioned that someday they all might meet.

She finished the letter, wishing her and child the very best of luck in the future.

Brenda never received a response.

At that time, the communists controlled incoming and outgoing correspondence from the western world. There would be no way of ever knowing whether Brenda's letter reached her despite her address being   available through the Polish newspaper.

CHAPTER FORTY

The two newly-wed couples began planning for their trip to America. Sabina-Belgian Airlines had offered to fly them, but they would have to go to Brussels to board the aircraft.

Sabina Air had offered to credit them the cost of the flight with a commitment to repay within twelve months, without interest.

New passports had to be arranged in a hurry. The British Government wanted to encourage immigrants to leave their over-crowded country.

Therefore, it became quite easy for temporary passport papers to become available.

They were delighted and excited, as Wednesday came to a close.

Thursday was their day of departure from Brussels and America was waiting for them.

The British Government had provided a bus to take them directly to the Brussels's airport.

They took with them very little, not that they had much to take. Left behind were Brenda's temporary family who had been so special to her and her friends, and the many new friends that they had made at work, in the government, at the Polish newspaper, and a host of other places during their short stay in England.

But they were ready for a new chance for a better life that could be waiting in America.

Sabina Airlines put the four of them into comfortable general seating in one of their converted military aircraft.

Six hours later they were to land into New York, at LaGuardia Field, not far from New York City itself.

CHAPTER
FORTY-ONE

The flight was long for them. They were prepared for a six-hour flight. Military c-rations were the only food offered during the ride, but a steward gave them plenty of drinks.

Elizabeth got air-sick. She was forced into the lavatory several times. (Later she was to learn that she was pregnant.)

United States Customs was set-up at the airport, expecting them.

Their passports did the trick.

No Polish-speaking interpreter was available. They had to wiggle their way through the usual inspections and interrogation that came with entry into the United States.

When they finished, one of the agents announced, "you need not go to Ellis Island. You've passed all that's required to enter our great country. Congratulations."

With that statement they knew that they had officially been welcomed into their new country.

Not knowing where to go, they approached an Army information table that was positioned near the airport entrance areas.

A young-looking American soldier offered to help them.

With a smile, Ivan told him of their desire to speak to an interpreter with Polish speaking skills. He promptly telephoned for one.

She arrived. Her name was Paula.

Paula had lived in Poland for nearly seven years before the war.

In perfect Polish, she commended them for bringing only light clothes and personal items.

"But we don't have any other items," Brenda responded.

Paula answered many questions that they needed to have answered.

She arranged for them to be driven to the east side of New York City where millions of immigrants were living at the time.

There, among the long list of multi-apartment complexes, were the graces of immigrant ghetto-type living.

The streets were full of people, vendors, vehicles, smoke, and plenty of noise. Yet the place seemed peaceful and probably safe.

This was their first sight of American freedom. They began to smile.

"We made it!" exclaimed Felix.

They were given a furnished apartment that belonged to the U.S. Army located in the midst of this overcrowded area.

Their temporary home was on the third floor of an old wooden building that had a plumber's shop underneath the apartments.

They were told that an interpreter-guide would be visiting them on the next day to help them find work and more permanent housing.

Paula was able to rearrange her schedule and volunteer to help the two young couples.

She used her connections to locate a better home for them just outside the Eastside overcrowded area.

The home had two bedrooms, a clean kitchen, and was handy to local transportation. They were thrilled.

The rent was being deferred for three months. The U.S. Government had offered dozens of these arrangements for special immigrants.

Paula had used favors to get them into this program.

On the second day, Felix was taken to a job in the warehouse of the Greater New York Sausage Company.

There he was taken under the wings of a Polish-speaking young man named Roberto. He was to receive slightly more than the current minimum wages of the day.

Roberto had been with the company for six years and was the assistant manager in the warehouse which employed ten others.

Felix and Roberto were to become close friends.

Elizabeth was brought to a local clinic where she was told of her pregnancy. She cried, but overall was delighted to be carrying Felix's baby. "I must tell him tonight. He will be happy, for sure."

CHAPTER FORTY-TWO

Ivan was brought to the construction company who had hired him and was responsible for all of them coming to the United States.

They immediately sent him to work on a new high-rise building being constructed behind Wall Street.

He was brought to the fourth floor by elevator and put to work, once again, taking bricks and cementing them to other bricks, as directed.

Brenda was offered a job with the U.S. Army corresponding with Polish executives that the military wanted to address for a sundry of reasons.

She graciously accepted the offer and was to enjoy the challenge they put before her.

Her pay was very respectable for the work that she contributed.

The two couples were now receiving monies that would afford them the chance to stay in New York and meet their rent and other needs.

Elizabeth was beginning to show her pregnancy and her clothes had to be expanded to meet the weight increase.

Felix and Elizabeth had decided to name their baby after Hyman.

Brenda and Ivan were absolutely thrilled to hear the news.

Elizabeth said, "if the baby is a girl, we will name her Helena. If the baby is a boy, we will name him Hyman."

Brenda promised to write to Juliette as soon as the baby was born.

The lives of the two young couples were improving day by day in America.

CHAPTER FORTY-THREE

Ivan began advancing in his job with the J.M. Bergen Construction Company. Mr. Bergen's wife was Polish. She had lost her family in the Second World War. They had met at Columbia University some fifteen years earlier.

John Bergen had fought in the war against the Nazis and when he heard of Ivan's background, they became quite close.

And to make it even more interesting, his wife had taught John enough Polish to speak in the language

John had expressed his disapproval for Jews in his business.

Ivan retaliated by saying, "my best friends are Jews and I am faithful to them in every respect. I was treated as a Jew during my capture by the Nazis. Please treat each person individually, not as a religion"

John was impressed with Ivan's message and assured him that in the future, he would treat each person individually, and he thanked him for the advice.

It wasn't long before Ivan was appointed manager of a new project where he was to win the favor of John Bergen and the company executives.

One of the Board of Directors of the company was taken with a stroke and could not continue to serve on the board.

Ivan was appointed by John to fill the position.

Four years later, John Bergen, now eighty-one, decided to retire to Florida.

He selected Ivan to become the Chairman of the Board and Chief Operating Officer of the firm.

His salary became enormous.

Their lawyers and accountants pushed the company onto Wall Street and made their stock available to the public.

Ivan was to become an important wealthy investor, holding stock in most of the major successful companies on the New York Stock Exchange.

Later, he was to serve on the Presidential Committee for Immigration in Washington, DC.

Brenda held her job for three years, then became pregnant with their first of four children.

She gave birth to three boys, Herbert (named after Hyman), Rowan, Kyle, and one girl, Helen (also named after Hyman).

The Ivan Kranopsky family had moved to western Connecticut where they built a large twelve-room estate in the Town of Devon.

Their oldest son Herbert had become a tennis star in high school and went on to play at Yale where he reached the collegiate national championship, only to lose in the finals to a little guy from Alabama State Institute.

Sons Rowan and Kyle both became accountants and joined large firms in the New York area.

Helen married Ronald Vanderbilt (not related to the famous Vanderbilt family).

Ronald's father was a broker on Wall Street and his mother was a doctor in a local clinic.

They produced two grandchildren for Ivan and Brenda to adore and spoil. Alexandria and Winston easily won over their doting grandparents.

The amazing story of Ivan and Brenda began to be published in many of the important newspapers and magazines in America.

CHAPTER
FORTY-FOUR

Elizabeth gave birth to baby Hyman. He was to be worshiped by both young couples. On his birthdays they would party, always remembering that he was named after their deceased friend.

Felix continued working at the Greater New York Sausage Company.

He, too, had worked his way up to the front office and had trained his replacement in the warehouse position that he had held.

The company widow, Sylvania Malone, had taken over the operations of the family business when her husband of twenty years had run away with his secretary to Cuba.

Sylvania had made peace with the Internal Revenue Service who after her husband's departure, left the company in tax debt that needed immediate addressing.

Felix comforted her with his clever ideas and personality. She would never forget his help during her time in need.

Finally, Felix was asked to run the business. His salary increase included an important list of benefits that he had never enjoyed before.

And run the business he did.

First, he increased the prices on their special tasting products.

Then he introduced a new type of sausage made from turkey processing and added flavor.

Felix called the line "The Hyman New Meat Division" using quality turkey meat from Pennsylvania and Delaware.

He also was instrumental in organizing the New York City Sausage Union which was to include some eighteen meat and sausage companies.

Felix wanted to buy together common ingredients and share some of the advertising costs of marketing.

Soon they were purchasing equipment together as well.

Then he devised a central office where all eighteen companies would share their administration duties, saving up to a million dollars a year and freeing up important floor space that many companies began using for added production.

The savings were divided equally among the eighteen companies.

Felix's story was featured at the International Business Convention held in Vienna, Austria. The publicity was to boost his popularity and the demand for his company's meat.

Felix and Elizabeth gave birth to another boy Windsor named after England's famous Royal family.

They enjoyed a lovely new home in upstate New Jersey where their children attended fine private schools.

Elizabeth convinced Felix to purchase a condominium in beautiful Newport, Rhode Island. They would spend the summers there for many years.

Their son Hyman graduated number one in his high school class and went on to Columbia to become a lawyer.

He became a partner in the firm of Haskell, Hogan & Hapstein in Manhattan.

Later he ran for the position of state representative and lost by only twelve votes.

His younger son Windsor skipped his junior and senior years at high school and became a professional baseball player.

Some five years later, he became a star hitter with the Cincinnati Reds in the National Professional Baseball League.

He was to spend eleven years in baseball and was voted into the Baseball Hall of Fame, at Cooperstown, New York.

Windsor later became chief of police in Scoberville, Pennsvlvania.

Felix and Elizabeth retired to Newport, Rhode Island, where Felix had purchased a small historic mansion along famous Ocean Drive.

In 2016, Felix passed away at age of eighty-eight.

Elizabeth, now eighty-seven, is still alive. She spends most of her time doting on her children and new grandchildren.

CHAPTER FORTY-FIVE

Before Felix passed away, the four of them flew to Poland. Pictures were taken at Hyman's Statue.

They attempted to locate Juliette and her child, without success. The local surviving Jewish community had lost track of her, and her child.

No one seemed to be aware that before Hyman's death, his wife, Juliette, and child had been sent to Siberia.

Their own home area had been totally destroyed during the war and parts of it had been rebuilt into a police training center.

They did visit the piece of Ivan's Catholic church, whose doors had become opened for surviving worshippers. There, Ivan, with his Jewish friends accompanying him, eloquently delivered an old Catholic blessing that brought tears to all who were present.

Their trip concluded with a visit to the train station, where regular transportation had returned to the area.

They chose to walk inside to view the remains of where they once sat, awaiting their assignments to the camps, that had been set-up by the conquering Nazis.

Once again, they were to realize that most of the individuals who had come through this station had not survived the war, and they knew how lucky they had been.

Back in America, Ivan rejoined the Catholic Church. He spent much of his time going to other churches and synagogues telling of his unusual early life story.

He volunteered, as a speaker, for many Jewish organizations and made several trips to Israel to share the story of his first-hand experiences of World War II where he had been "treated as a Jew."

Ivan is now ninety years-old and is in reasonably good health.

The love of his life, Brenda, passed away three months earlier from a rare disease.

Before she died, she wrote this story in Polish and became a well- known author.

Her beauty remains in Ivan's everyday thoughts.

In the year 2012, Ivan established a trust in Brenda's name leaving twelve million dollars to the homeless.

Ivan frequently visits Newport, Rhode Island, where he meets up with Elizabeth and they visit Felix's gravesite.

In Polish they say, "We will always remember you and the others."

God Bless.

AUTHOR'S NOTE

The world became different after the Second World War concluded.

Peace, though fragile, was thought to be evident.

The story of Ivan Kranopsky could have happened.

So many stories came from that terrible war, many that have never been told.

Maybe this novella will encourage others who know, or have survived, to share their experiences with the rest of the world.

Hopefully, stories like this will never happen again.

ABOUT THE AUTHOR

 A life-long Rhode Islander, Burt was raised in Providence and Pawtucket in a family with a diverse musical presence that inspired him to pursue the piano, trumpet, baritone horn and vocals, and develop a profound love for jazz.

The former owner of several successful businesses throughout New England, Burt is now retired and lives in Cranston, Rhode Island.

Burt is also the author of *'Round Newport: Recalling 60 years of Jazz Around Newport, RI*, *Discovering Newport*, *Breakfast with Jackie O and Other Stories* and *Capmaker for the Czar: An Immigrant's Story*

PHOTO CREDITS

All photographs used in this book are in the public domain.

Page 3: Possibly a return to a destroyed village after WWII, Date: Between 1939 and 1945, Source English: Image printed in the 60's from Polish Archive negative and distributed by the Archive, now in Marek Tuszyński's collection of WWII prints. Scan by Jarekt from 5 × 8 cm print. Pencil number 391 in the back. Author: Unknown.

Page 7: Unknown (Franz Konrad confessed to taking some of the photographs, the rest was probably taken by photographers from Propaganda Kompanie nr 689.[5][6]) - This is a retouched picture, which means that it has been digitally altered from its original version. Modifications: artifacts and scratches removed, levels adjusted, and image sharpened. Stroop Report - Warsaw Ghetto Uprising 06.jpg. Modifications made by Durova. Created: between 19 April 1943 and 16 May 1943 .

Page 31: Jews from Carpathian Ruthenia arrive at Auschwitz, offloaded onto the ramp at Birkenau in close proximity to the gas chambers. The chimneys in the background belong to Crematoria II and III on the left and right respectively, whose structures house subterranean undressing and gassing rooms. The photograph is part of the collection known as the Auschwitz Album. Date: May or June 1944, Auschwitz-Birkenau, Poland. Source: Yad Vashem. The album was donated to Yad Vashem by Lili Jacob, a survivor, who found it in the Mittelbau-Dora concentration camp in 1945. Author Unknown. Several sources believe the photographer to have been Ernst Hoffmann or Bernhard Walter of the SS.

Page 49: Striped uniform of a Belgian political prisoner (denoted by the "B" in a red triangle) in Dachau concentration camp. In the National Museum of the Resistance, Anderlecht. Date: 5 September 2013, 14:02:21. Author: Brigade Piron.

Page 76: Author Ashley Van Haeften Drachenburg and Konigswinter, the Rhine, Germany-LCCN2002714097

Page 84: WWII: Europe: France; "Into the Jaws of Death — U.S. Troops wading through water and Nazi gunfire", circa 1944-06-06. Chief Photographer's Mate (CPHoM) Robert F. Sargent. Description: A LCVP (Landing Craft, Vehicle, Personnel) from the U.S. Coast Guard-manned USS Samuel Chase disembarks troops of Company E, 16th Infantry, 1st Infantry Division (the Big Red One) wading onto the Fox Green section of Omaha Beach (Calvados, Basse-Normandie, France) on the morning of June 6, 1944. American soldiers encountered the newly formed German 352nd Division when landing. During the initial landing two-thirds of Company E became casualties. Date: 6 June 1944, 08:30.

Page 88: Panzer IV and a Tiger I of the Panzer Lehr division at Villers-Bocage.

Page 108: German officer in ruins of Warsaw after Warsaw Uprising. Date: circa 1944. Source: Image printed in the 60's from Polish Archive negative and distributed by the Archive, now in Marek Tuszyński's collection of WWII prints. Scan by Jarekt from 5 × 8 cm print. Author: Unknown.

PAGE 182: Digital ID: 482579. Abbott, Berenice -- Photographer. October 28, 1935. Modern Vision #57 Festive lights in curlicue designs arch over street, men with tall ladder, wagons, cars, billboards; 'el' and Municipal Bldg. just visible.. .Source: Changing New York / Berenice Abbott. http://digitalgallery.nypl.org/nypldigital/id?482579.

Made in the USA
Middletown, DE
01 March 2019